Owned By The Freshman

a Brazen Boys story

by Daryl Banner

Books By Daryl Banner

The Beautiful Dead Trilogy:
    The Beautiful Dead *(Book 1)*
    Dead Of Winter *(Book 2)*
    Almost Alive *(Book 3)*

The OUTLIER Series:
    Outlier: Rebellion *(Book 1)*
    Outlier: Legacy *(Book 2)*
    Outlier: Reign Of Madness *(Book 3)*
    Outlier: Beyond Oblivion *(Book 4)*
    Outlier: Five Kings *(Book 5)*

The Brazen Boys:
A series of standalone M/M romance novellas.
    Dorm Game *(Book 1)*
    On The Edge *(Book 2)*
    Owned By The Freshman *(Book 3)*
    Dog Tags *(Book 4)*

Other Books by Daryl Banner:
    super psycho future killers
    Psychology Of Want
    Love And Other Bad Ideas
        (a collection of seven short plays)

Owned By The Freshman: a Brazen Boys story

Copyright © 2015 by Daryl Banner

All rights reserved.

No part of this publication may be used or reproduced in any manner whatsoever, including but not limited to being stored in a retrieval system or transmitted in any form or by any means, electronic, mechanical, photocopying, recording or otherwise, without the written permission of the author.

This book is a work of fiction.
Names, characters, groups, businesses, and incidents either are the product of the author's imagination or are used fictitiously. Any resemblance to actual places or persons, living or dead, is entirely coincidental.

Cover & Interior Design : Daryl Banner

Cover Model : Nick Duffy
www.instagram.com/nickduffyfitness

Photo of Nick Duffy by Simon Barnes

Owned By The Freshman

a Brazen Boys story

by Daryl Banner

[1]

He's such a cocky fucker.

You know the type. He's hot shit and he knows it. Overconfident. Strutting to class, he's surrounded by his bros. His snug, hot shit clothes show off all the best parts of his body, which is perfectly proportionate and an obvious result of daily trips to the gym—or he's got perfect genes, which is somehow just as likely. He kicks up his feet in my classroom, sporting his bright red-and-white high tops. Carefree and above it all, this tool. Even his hair's cocky, swept up into a proud little tuft in the front.

What a cocky shit.

Owned By The Freshman

I hardly notice any of my other students, so distracted by that freshman in the back row. My classroom is the small black box theater, which is an improvement from the cramped room they gave me in the Communications building for the last two years during the renovation. The black box has raked seating on three sides of the acting area, which is really just a square of space we refer to as the stage. My students occupy one of the three seating areas while the other two are empty, except for the one chair I'm in, flanked by my director's notebook and my box of script sides and props. I don't know why I brought my box of props on the first day; we never use them.

I twist my wrist and find we're five past ten. I glance down at my roll sheet, noting that twenty out of the thirty in this room are actual Theatre or Dance majors. At least the majority of these fools will take my class seriously.

As for Mister Hot Shit in the back row, he'd better participate or else he will not be passing my course, I can guarantee that.

"Everyone here?" I call out, rising from my seat and inspiring all the murmurs of the students to draw to a soundless vacuum. "You are in eleven-o-one: Intro To Basic Acting. Movement, Voice, and Stage Combat, eleven-ten, eleven-twenty and twenty-ten respectively, are down the hall in the rehearsal room—in case you're lost. Intro To General Theatre Studies is in the main auditorium. As there are thirty present and thirty registered to take this class, I'll assume we're all in the right place. Am I safe to assume that?"

Blank stares meet mine. Great.

"I'm your professor," I go on, "and I am *not* an easy A. You will work for your grade in here and I expect you ... *all of you* ... to participate. We're going to jump into our first exercise. I want you, one by one, to come here to the stage and introduce yourself to your peers." I stroll back to my seat, sit and, with half-opened eyes, survey the students patiently and add: "First one up doesn't get brownie points, but I *always* remember who's first."

No one moves, except for their heads as they look at one another wondering who's daring to go first. I wonder if my reputation for being a hard-ass acting professor is preceding me, judging from their eyes. The nerves and freshmen fear is as visible as a mist, able to be tasted on the tongue.

The hot shit in the back, in stark contrast to the rest of the class, doesn't look worried in the least; his feet kicked up, his mouth twisted into a smirk that I daresay looks *bored*, he brings his hands behind his head and yawns.

"We could wait here all day," I say calmly, though I know my words inspire fear anyway. "It's your first-ever acting lesson: learning how to introduce yourself. Even if you never go on to be an actor or pursue a job in the acting field, you'll still remember the lessons of this class in some future job interview, or in your board meetings and presentations, or even when you go on a date with that guy who looks nothing like his profile pic." I slap the attendance chart onto my lap. "Let's get introduced, people."

Finally, a spritely young female gets up from the front row and turns to face the class. She speaks with a spine-grating, nasally voice that I'm sure Mr. Harrington, the voice teacher down the hall, is going to have a party fixing.

Once the ice is broken, the rest of the class introduce themselves one by one, more and more eager with each passing student. Some of them are quite funny, inspiring laughs from the others with their quirks and snarky quips. One at a time, I mark them off so as to keep track, noting the Theatre majors.

Soon, there's just one left. Of course it'd be him; so above the class, he can't bother with this simple assignment. I've only been teaching for five years, but I have about eight years of college in my brain and I know his type all too well. I've seen this kind of guy, over and over.

"One more left," I announce, narrowing my eyes to focus on the freshman in the back.

His name must be Justin Brady, according to my student roster and a simple process of elimination. He's nineteen. Undeclared major.

I'm guessing he's only here for the required Fine Arts credit. This Justin Brady doesn't have an inch of interest in acting. He must think it's some blow-off credit. Just look at him. He's had his feet kicked up the whole time, his arms slung over the backs of the seats next to him. He's already over it; I can see it in his glassy, lazy eyes. He's just waiting for the semester to end so he can snatch his A or B based on his good looks and charm. *You're going to need more than good looks to get through me, Mr. Brady.*

"Justin Brady," I announce. "You're up."

As if casually rising from the chair to fetch a can of soda from the fridge, he slowly hops down the steps, runs a hand through his short, messy hair, then stands before his peers.

"Hi," he says flippantly. "I'm from Austin. I'm nineteen. I like cars, they're pretty badass. Gets you from one place to another, which is convenient." The words just roll off his tongue like a mindless joke, like thoughtless rambling. He couldn't give less of a fuck. "That's me."

"How about a name?" I ask coolly.

"You already introduced me," he says in a tone that suggests I'm an idiot.

"I'm not going to be at your job interviews or your board meetings or your dates," I say, with just as similar a tone. "So, unless you plan for me to be there to introduce you, I suggest learning how to do it yourself."

The class ruffles a bit at my reply, a meek titter or chuckle here and there. Justin, despite it, remains entirely unfazed. He thrusts his hands into his pockets, the muscles in his arms flexing as he does, and his half-opened eyes turn to me. His eyebrows are lifted and pulled together, crinkling up his forehead.

"We're waiting," I state calmly. "By all means, continue."

He faces his peers. "I'm from Austin. I like cars. My name is Justin Brady." He turns his face, lifting an eyebrow as if to ask whether or not that's what I wanted. When all I return is a deadpan stare, he figures his obligation to be done and carelessly hops up the stairs, swinging into his back row seat at the top.

I can't say I'm proud that I was spot-on about that cocky little shit. A part of me, albeit buried deep down in the murky recesses of my cynical being, was kind of hoping I was wrong and that the hot shit kid in the back row would actually turn out to be my star student. Every now and then, I do *enjoy* to be proven wrong.

Oh well. Wouldn't be the first time I was let down. I rise from my chair and face the class myself. "My name is Thomas Kozlowski. Call me Professor Kozlowski, or just Thom will do. I performed in New York City off-Broadway for two years after my undergrad, then returned promptly to finish my master's. I've taught acting for five years. Don't let my youthful face deceive you; I'm older than I look."

No one laughs. No one ever does. I wonder why I still use that same lame joke.

"I may already have a certain reputation for being intimidating and strict, but I assure you, if you participate and give me everything you got, I can be your best friend." I study them. "You *want* me to be your best friend."

They share the same look all my students have on their first day after my little speech: scared and silent and sheet white. I will ignore the obvious exception in the back row. He'll have it coming; that much I can guarantee.

"I don't tolerate tardiness, except for this first day when freshmen are finding their way. As none of you were late, I'll assume you all found your way well enough. Every morning at ten, the doors to this theater will be locked, and you will not be permitted in if you are late. I look forward to seeing you for an hour every Monday, Wednesday, and Friday morning at ten o'clock. I expect you to choose, work on, and have memorized four dramatic monologues that you will work on for most of the semester. Each one must be no longer than 25 seconds. Next class, we do exercises. Dismissed."

The students take a solid ten seconds to gather themselves, their eyes wide and their nervous systems thoroughly provoked. That's just the way I like to see them on the first day.

I'd expect nothing less.

Without waiting, I toss my notebooks into the box of props, then carry it out of the auditorium. I make a special effort *not* to pay witness to the cocky back row freshman strolling out of the class ahead of me, backpack slung over his shoulder.

I reach my office, drop the box onto a table, then lift my gaze to find the short, thirty-something voice professor seated at my desk.

"Harrington," I say shortly.

"Done your terrorizing for the day?" He chuckles lightly, twirling a pencil between his stubby pale fingers—one of *my* pencils. "Never mind, I already know the answer. Seriously, Thom, these stiff formalities, gross. My name's Jeff, please use it."

"*Jeff.*" I cross my arms. "That's my desk."

"And it's comfier than mine. How do you like your babies this semester?"

I make a choice to be kind and friendly for a moment. "Hmm. Too soon to tell, I guess. How do you like yours?"

"Abysmal. Hey, wanna grab some lunch?"

Moment's over. "What do you want, Jeff?"

Jeff drops his jaw, playing offended and drawing a limp hand to his chest. He's got his contacts in today, so his light blue eyes sparkle. "My feelings! Ouch! You sting me so!"

He doesn't look a day over twenty-five. We're the youngest professors, and ever since I started teaching, he's clung to me desperately. Our pesky colleagues insist that because we're both young, gay, and single, we obviously are meant to hook up. But if there's anything anyone knows about me, it's that I don't like to be told what to do ... or *who* to do.

"And I'll sting you again." I move to a cabinet, stowing away folders and pulling new ones for my afternoon advanced acting classes: Improv at one o'clock, then Emotional Truth at three. Those classes are only twice a week, hour-and-a-half, making my Fridays mercifully short. "You here to ask to trade classrooms already?"

"No, no. Much prefer the rehearsal room. The black box is too ... stark."

"Funny. I find the rehearsal room stark." I slam shut the cabinet, flipping open my folder to remind myself how many students I have in Improv. Damn, only eleven?

"Let's grab some lunch."

"Not hungry."

"You don't have any first years you want to despair about? C'mon, Thom. It's basically our tradition to sit over college fast food on the first day and spill our woes."

There is the subject of one particularly cocky freshman I could chew and spit out, but I'd rather not. "We've never done it before."

"Hmm. Your point?"

"You can't call something 'our tradition' if we haven't even done it once, Mr. Harrington. You're still in my chair."

"Name's Jeff, and your chair's cozy. So let's *make* it a tradition! Starting today." He leans forward, smiling stupidly. "Tell me which of your fish you're gonna fry this year."

Jeff's always had a kind smile. Why am I so awful to him? "His name's Justin Brady."

That's the name that's on my lips later, when the sun's fallen and my shower's had and I'm lying naked in bed. I move a hand beneath the sheets and I imagine an empty auditorium. I'm at the back, coming up the aisle. There's a sexy guy on the edge of the stage in this dream, his legs dangling, his biceps bulging, his hair perfect. "Justin Brady," I whisper aloud, filling my bedroom with his name, moving my hand. I draw closer and closer to him, my heartbeat in my ears. His eyes have tiny flames in them, like some exotic fire demon. When I reach the stage, I put myself between his legs because I belong there. "Justin Brady." His red-and-white high tops glow. His sexy smile spreads across that flawless face of his ... that flawless, smooth skin. I listen to him breathe—his little lifts and falls of breath are all I can hear. Or maybe it's my own as I lie in this bed jerking off. "Justin Brady." He doesn't move from the edge of that stage and he doesn't have to; I lean forward and put my lips against his. I can do this because it's a dream, because it's not real, because I'm living in the fantasy world of a play in my mind. It's a play without lines, a play where Justin Brady and I are the only characters. Fuck all the others who might've been cast in this role. Fuck all the others who would've beaten me in an audition ... This is *my* moment.

Our lips are locked in a kiss that's more powerful, more fierce, more heartrending than any kiss in real life could ever strive to be. I feel the force of his *jaw* in the kiss. I feel his nose as it breathes against my cheek.

I feel his heat like a hundred candles.

"Justin Brady," I whisper into the night. I'm so close, but I hold off; I want this to last for hours ... I want to lose sleep over this boy.

Suddenly I'm on top of him, exploring every inch of his muscled body. "Justin Brady." My mischievous hands find his firm biceps, his chiseled abs, his pecs with their pointy kisses for nipples. "Justin." I push my mouth on his again, grinding my hips against his. "Brady." Our cocks wrestle through the thick fabric of our jeans, pushing a pleasant sickness through my being. I've never wanted anything so badly. All my life I've been shut away. All my life, roleplaying, acting, observing ... For just this one moment, for just this one beautiful boy, I don't want to act anymore. I want to live it.

"Justin Brady."

Abruptly, the kissing ends. His eyes open—smart, keen, hazel eyes—and his mouth spreads into the biggest shit-eating grin. His lips wet, cheeks flushed, teeth shining and bright ...

He whispers: "I own you."

And then I cum.

[2]

The weeks seem to drift like dreams. For the first few weeks, I take my Basic Acting students through exercises and script-reading skills. Baby steps. I literally feel like I'm teaching them to read. "This is what a character is," I hear myself say. "Find your motivation."

"Don't highlight your lines," I say once. "Every word uttered by every other character is important and vital. Highlighting your lines tells your brain that the only important thing in this play is you and your pretty face. 'Oh hey, look at me, I'm so fucking important.' If I see a highlighted script, I'm burning it."

Through the simple exercises, I have them stand in front of the rest of the class. One exercise involves them telling a personal story and the class having to decide whether it's made-up or real.

I take deep pleasure each time it's Justin Brady's turn. He always takes the stage like he already owns it, but when he starts to perform, I spot and take note of a hundred different things to fix. I feel stings of pride when I see his flaws, no matter how pretty he is.

Each time he finishes, he gives me a piercing look, then smiles like the cat that's just caught the fish. "Joke's on you," I mutter once under my breath after class. "*You're* the fish."

On Tuesdays and Thursdays, I don't have but one advanced acting class to teach, so I have lots of time to plan and catch up on paperwork before the evening rehearsals. Auditions for the first shows have already come and gone, but I'm unconcerned, as I don't have a show to direct until the spring, and *my* auditions aren't until the end of October.

It's one of these lazy Tuesdays that I'm troubling over a half-eaten sandwich and an unopened bottle of Diet Coke in the University Center cafeteria. I think it's October already, but can't be sure; might still be the end of September. "Has it really already been a month?" I ask my half-eaten sandwich. I feel a ball of sadness, thinking about the freshman again. *You're so obsessed*, I tell myself, annoyed. I'm sad because I realize I only have a few more months with him and then he'll be gone. Fine Arts credit nabbed, he'll move on and I'll never see his pretty face again. *There will be other pretty faces*, I reason with myself. *Hotter faces. Older faces. More appropriate faces to lust after.*

Then again, with his current inability to take my class seriously, I wonder if I'll even pass him at all. Unbeknownst to him, I've already given him two F's and a D on some of his exercises. He doesn't give a fuck, he makes light of everything, and he isn't affected in the least by my warnings and criticisms.

You're so obsessed, I repeat to myself.

And I'm also fuming over the fact that I wasn't permitted to direct the show I'd wanted to direct, but instead pushed to take some old, tired piece of work that everyone's seen a thousand times. I'm so sick of the same shit regurgitated over and over again. I'm so fucking bored. Maybe that's why I need Justin Brady.

Maybe that's why I cling to the freshman in Basic Acting. He's something new. He's … given me cause to masturbate like a machine countless times a week. He makes me feel alive.

"I own you," he said in my dreams.

Bitter and bugged and bored, my stomach does a backflip when, quite unexpectedly, I spot him across the cafeteria: Justin Brady, the carefree freshman. What draws my attention is the obnoxious laughter spilling from his mouth as he sits at a table among his bros. Of course he'd be sitting at a table among his bros. His arms thrown over the back of the booth he's in, he's telling his friends some story I can't hear, and they all listen, leaned forward with bright, expectant smiles on their stupid, eighteen-or-nineteen-year-old faces. When he delivers the punch line, all his buds explode into laughter, cheering him on and slapping their hands and spraying food like a bunch of monkeys.

Just as he finishes his story, he looks up and, under an upward tuft of brown spiky hair, Justin's smart, sharp eyes find mine.

I look down at my half-eaten sandwich that I'd given up on half an hour ago, annoyed that he caught me looking. I don't like giving people like him the satisfaction of knowing that he just got the attention he so clearly lives for.

Not that I've been jerking off like mad to thoughts of him. Not that, in my dreams, I've pushed my lips against his and ran my fingers down his rippled, smooth body.

Stop thinking on the dreams, I tell myself, *or you'll give yourself a boner.*

I hear another explosion of laughter and clapping, but I don't look up. I just roll my eyes and lift the tasteless sandwich to my face. I'm not sure what it is about me and know-it-all freshmen. Maybe it reminds me too much of when I was a first year in the Theatre program, surrounded by loudmouthed morons who got all the attention and the friends and the roles. Those "cool cats", those top-of-the-class cocky motherfuckers ... They always got everything they wanted just because they're *louder*. Boys with voices. I was the one who faded into the crowd like human camouflage.

Is that why I've become so bitter as an adult? I can't even eat a sandwich without criticizing it. Seriously, I'd asked for no pickles and they fucking put pickles. Does anyone *listen* anymore, or is everyone so busy being loud and voiced and noticed?

"Hey, teach."

I look up, startled to find Justin Brady standing there in front of me. His hands are shoved into the pockets of his faded, acid-washed white-belted designer jeans, causing the biceps in his taut arms to bulge against his snug heather grey t-shirt. His beady hazel eyes, keen as a dog's, study me as I study him. His lips are pouty and deceptively innocent—like he's never up to anything. His nose is like a button, his cheeks are flushed with boyish fervor, and his eyebrows are pushed up expectantly, wrinkling his forehead into a spread of adorable creases.

He's the guy I'd never dare approach back in college. He's exactly the type of adorable, flashy, attention-stealing guy I'd pray I got the pleasure of sitting next to in all my classes, even if he was straight and never looked at me. He's the guy I'd pray to have as a roommate, or a lab partner, or to be cast with in some steamy gay scene where we'd have to practice kissing all the time. Just the fantasy of that threatens to give me a boner under the table.

"Do you need something?" I ask, my eyes lingering at his shoulders, somehow unable to meet the intensity of his staring.

"No. Just looking forward to class this week. Found a really good dialogue." He smiles proudly.

I roll my eyes. "It's *monologue*," I explain less than patiently, "as it's just with one person. A *dialogue* is between *two* people."

I corrected him in class already. Twice. To my words, he just grins and says: "A dialogue. Like ... what *we're* having."

I finally meet his gaze. It's crushing, the way he looks down at me with that cocky smirk on his face. It's humiliating to even admit it to myself, what this guy can do with just a curve of his smug, hot shit lips.

Dream-Justin whispers: "*I own you.*"

"Like what we're having," I agree quietly.

Justin grins, showing his bright, white, perfect teeth. "I'll see you tomorrow, teach." And, quick as that, he strolls back to his table across the way to rejoin his friends who, I only now notice, were watching our exchange.

My face flushes and I stare back down at my sandwich, forcing myself to take a hefty bite from it—a bite from which I nearly choke. I even have to open the bottle of Diet Coke I was planning to save for later, swigging until I stop gagging on the bite that won't quite go down. What a fitting and ironic predicament, to have bitten off more than I can chew.

Owned By The Freshman

After the choking, I start to eat more calmly, and I find my mind wandering. I think about some imaginary boy I might've met many years ago in my freshman year. I imagine some made-up scenario where we might've been assigned as partners in an acting scene. In the scene, we'd be required to take off each other's clothes, to touch each other's bodies, and to join our lips. In the fantasy, we both insist we have to rehearse the scene over and over and over again, rehearse it repeatedly until it's absolutely right, until it's absolutely perfect.

Under the table, my cock is throbbing. It's my horny little secret, and I writhe in silent, solitary torment as I think on my fantasy and the sexy scene and the beautiful acting partner with which I've been matched.

But rehearsals always end, and then all too soon it's time for the show, and we all know that when the show ends, so does the fantasy.

[3]

I stroll into the black box promptly at ten o'clock that Wednesday morning and lock the doors behind me. I hear the muted chatter of the students draw to perfect silence as I enter. To their surprise, I don't sit on my own in the side seating, but instead sit among them, taking a chair two to the left of the nasally girl and directly in front of a very specific someone else, whose red-and-white high tops are kicked up on the back of the chair next to mine.

"Shoes, Mr. Brady. Respect the seats or no one will." He pulls his feet off the back. I feel a tiny pinch of victory. "So, who's up first?"

For one tense, lovely moment, no one stirs. Today is their first day of "real" acting, after a month and a half of exercises and techniques and vocabulary. Every student expects someone else to get up and be brave. Either that, or no one actually has a monologue prepared. That's also just as likely; I've certainly had first year classes in the past where no one was ready on the first day. I remember asking for someone to do their monologue but twice, then getting up and leaving, declaring the students failed for the day. It left a lasting impression ... that one simple thing I did ... and from thereafter, I seemed to have earned myself a reputation.

"No one?" I say, testing them. I look to the left at all the startled faces. I look to the right. "No one at all?"

"I'll go," someone says, then rises from his seat and hops down the steps.

It's Justin Brady. I'm genuinely surprised. I peek down at my student roster, marking his name. "Interesting," I say aloud, making sure the others hear me. "Interesting that the first one up is not even a Theatre major." Maybe I had Justin all wrong. Maybe he's got a shot.

I bring my eyes to meet Mr. Brady's as he stands in front of the class. He's wearing a plain white tee today, still somehow making it look like this perfect and deliberate choice, as it fits him so perfectly and shows off his arms. His jeans are acid-washed and he wears a red-and-white striped belt, matching his high tops. His swept-up tuft of brown hair gives him a look of proudness, or maybe it's just that hint of a smirk on his lips.

I own you.

"You begin by telling us your name," I say, presuming to instruct him, as he is not a major, never done an audition, and might not know the protocol. "Just like if you were auditioning. State the name of the play your monologue is from, the playwright, and then just begin."

He lifts an eyebrow, his forehead wrinkling cutely. "Justin Brady," he announces. "Uh ... I think the play's called ... *Swag*. And playwright is Bobby Fischer."

I'm about to protest that I've never heard of that play nor playwright when suddenly Justin lifts his shirt over his head, whipping it off.

A tiny score of gasps and titters shiver across the classroom at the sight of Justin as he pulls off his shirt, revealing a slender, smooth, toned body of muscular perfection. His pecs look like they never rest, perky and firm to the eye, his nipples pink and small. His subtle stretch of abs lead to a light dusting of hair that draws a line down his tiny belly button and vanishes down the lip of his low-hanging jeans.

"You can't take off your shirt," I blurt out.

Justin looks confused. "But it's part of the monologue. The ... The character is shirtless."

"We're not doing this in *costume*," I argue back, my eyes drifting to his perfect nipples, to his toned obliques, to his plump arms. I can't believe this is happening and I can't believe I'm trying to stop it from happening. "P-Put your shirt back on."

"Aren't we acting, though?" His face is wrinkled, innocent, the shirt bunched up in his hands like a football, which makes his biceps bulge deliciously. Ugh, listen to me: *deliciously*.

"Please let him do it shirtless," utters a girl.

The class breaks into a short-lived bout of chuckles and snickering, then falls back into silence. Justin stands there like some ridiculous teen model, waiting for my go-ahead.

I feel so undermined. After two months of training their minds one way, the students are suddenly learning a lesson from Justin's display today, that they can just do what they want, that there's no order or fear or practice in the Theatre world. The most potent force that trained me to be who I am today is *fear*; if they don't learn that, then I've failed them.

Justin, self-proclaimed icon of fearlessness, gives a little shrug, assuming he'd won, then tosses his shirt into an empty seat in the front row. He stands before us, despite my mouth still being parted with my next unspoken words on my tongue, and begins his piece:

"All the boys look at me," he says, his face mirroring the smugness of his words, looking smart and self-important. "I know they do. All the boys look at me and they see just another hot boy in the ... club. But I'm more than that. I'm more than what they see." He delivers the monologue to someone in the front row, and a very humiliating part of me, a private, buried-deep-down, secret part of me wishes he were delivering the words to me.

Justin lifts his gaze, focusing on someone else now. "I'm more than just the boy in front of you. I'm also smart. I'm also kind and caring. I'm generous and, if any of those other boys think they can be me, I'll tell you what, they sure got some big shoes to fill."

He looks at someone else. "Because I got *swag*." Then Justin gives a wink and flashes a grin, then turns his attention to me, eyebrows lifted. "Done," he announces.

A light applause starts to happen, which sends an annoyed shiver through my body. "This isn't a *performance*," I say, cutting off the gentle applause as if it were the most offensive thing in the world. "This is a *classroom*."

"How'd I do?" he asks bluntly.

I frown at him, narrowing my eyes and forcing myself to ignore the fact that I'm addressing the sexy shirtless nineteen-year-old that I've been fantasizing about for over a month. "For one, that piece is just ... terrible. Bad writing ... No meat ... Ugh. I recommend finding something else if you want to actually learn anything about acting this semester. Two, unless you're giving a sermon, which I don't suspect you are, you need to focus on *one* person during your monologue, as it is a short speech you're giving to someone else. Three—"

"Oh, like a *dia*logue, except without the other person," he says with a smart smirk.

"Like a dialogue without the other person. Three, your piece is too long. 34 seconds. Needs to be under 25 like I explained last class. You take so many pauses between your sentences I can drive an eighteen-wheeler through them. And next time, I want you to keep your shirt on and take the art of acting seriously, or else I guarantee you will flunk my class. Got it?"

He doesn't look daunted in the least. In fact, I daresay my spiel gave his spine cause to straighten and his smirk cause to become a shit-eating grin. "Got it, teach."

"Professor Kozlowski," I correct him, a bit harsher than I might've intended. "You can put your shirt back on now."

Unhurriedly, he nabs his shirt from the chair in the front row, winking at someone, then returns all the way to the back row before bothering to put it on. I don't even watch him, as he's behind me now, and simply listen to the soft ruffling of the t-shirt as it slips back on his body, putting away all his spectacular gifts.

Spectacular gifts. I'm such a joke.

"Next," I mutter tiredly.

After a moment of uncertainty, the nasally girl rises from her seat and takes to the front. She introduces herself, introduces her piece, then soars right into it proudly. I prop up my chin with a lazy hand and watch with half-opened eyes. She finishes and I hardly have a thing to say. She sits back down and another takes her place, some guy from the front whose thick beard can't hide the fear in his eyes.

Good. Be afraid.

On and on the class goes, monologue after monologue, student after student, and I issue them each a handful of words for a critique. During the eleventh monologue, I feel a stab of shame, as if I'm letting down my students because I can't seem to pull my dirty mind away from the striking image of Justin Brady, shirtless, cocky, delivering his monologue to the class. I'm doing all these students an injustice because of my utter inability to focus on something other than my undue horniness.

As if on cue, his shoes come to rest on the back of the chair next to me. I flinch, seconds from saying something, then let it slide, not bothering. I've let him take enough of my attention for a day.

"That's all we have time for today," I state. "Rest of you will go Friday. Since you'll have another day to prepare and to learn from the mistakes of your peers, I expect you to be better than them. Oh, and don't forget, auditions for my spring show are tomorrow evening at 8 in the main auditorium. Sign-up sheet is posted in the green room."

As the students gather their things and start to leave, I lift my chin at the cocky freshman passing by. "Oh, and Mr. Brady ..."

He stops, turns and lifts an eyebrow.

"As your piece was so far off the mark," I tell him, "You'll go *again* on Friday. And I expect you to do better. I warned you on your first day that I wasn't an easy A."

The freshman gives one simple nod, his mouth opening into a spread of bright white teeth, flashing, then he saunters out of the black box, the door and the light cutting off abruptly as it slams shut.

I swallow hard, thinking on the countless nights I've jerked off, thinking of Justin Brady. *I own you*, Dream-Justin whispers in my ear.

I own you.

[4]

When I'm eating lunch on Thursday, I sit in the exact same spot as I did Tuesday and I stare at another half-eaten sandwich, except across the cafeteria, there is no freshman.

I don't know what I expected.

I feel ashamed and guilty and dumb, for allowing my insubordinate heart to thrash and jump and dance for a nineteen-year-old idiot with flashy teeth and a rocking body.

The sun melts behind the skyline of college buildings and dormitories, and I stroll into the main auditorium and find my place in the second row, preparing my notebook for the soon-to-come onslaught of student hopefuls wishing to be in one of the spring main-stage shows. I spot Mr. Harrington, seated at the opposite end of the row. He gives me a tiny wave. I return him a blank stare, then turn my gaze to the stage, ready and waiting.

The stage assistant brings in the first wave of auditions one at a time. They're all boring at best. "Next," I keep hearing myself saying, and the next one is ushered in to perform their required 25-second dramatic and 25-second comedic pieces. Some of the returning second-years and third-years perform their usual, decent monologues. I don't even have to take notes, remembering most of them by name and by the roles they had in last year's productions.

Before the second wave, Mr. Harrington moves to the seat next to me. "Anyone good?"

I shrug. "Same old, same old."

"Our Juliet from last year's really improved on her enunciation," he remarks, I assume taking all the credit, being the voice guru. "You can tell with the way she says *Capulet*."

"Too bad her Romeo's a one-note dud." I draw a line across the page, frowning. "Next," I call out to the assistant at the end of the stage.

"Not everyone can be a love story," he points out.

"Please. *Romeo and Juliet* is not a love story. *Romeo and Juliet* is about two horny teenagers making dumb decisions."

When I notice the face of our next audition, my insides turn cold and hot all at once. He stands center stage and, when I get a look at his face, I realize he's *not* who I thought he was and breathe a discreet sigh of relief.

Not discreet enough for my buddy. "What is it?" asks Mr. Harrington.

"Nothing." I readjust the clipboard on my lap, itch a spot on my head and clear my throat. I really wish thoughts and fears of that puffed-up kid from Basic Acting would quit intruding on every part of my every day this semester. Or maybe I don't wish that at all, who knows. Am I really this lonely, that I would let my mind and heart chase after a kid half my age?

Okay, to be fair, he's about two-thirds my age. But I still have ten years on the fucker.

Halfway through the audition of the sorta-looks-like-Justin-but-isn't guy, Mr. Harrington leans into me and says, "Maybe after auditions, wanna grab a bite? I'm kinda craving eggrolls."

"No, Mr. Harrington. I have a project for my advanced acting class to prepare," I lie.

"Project? You still do those?"

"My students are playing a game," I decide just now. "They interview their acting partner, in-character, and write reports on what they believe and what they don't believe."

Mr. Harrington leans into me even more, his shoulder pushing against mine and his breath reeking of spearmint. "Sometimes, you gotta just let go, know what I mean?" *No, I don't know what you mean, Jeff.* I bother to think it, straining to focus on the kid onstage. "Like, you gotta give in and kinda just *go for it*, you get me, Thom? Keep making excuses instead of just grabbing a bite with me, keep holding back and, like, eventually—"

"Thank you," says the kid onstage, then leaves. I demonstratively take notes.

Jeff sighs, collapsing back into his seat and giving up on me. *Just go for it*, he says. *Let go.* He has no idea what the fuck he's asking me to do, with all his advice and knowhow of life. He has no idea who I am, other than the "other young professor" and resident bitter bunny.

If only he knew my obsessive, unseeable hunger below the waist. If only he knew …

"Hmm," hums Lesandra to my other side, the sixty-or-so-year-old head of the costume department. "I could dress up that sexy little man in a show or three." Chewing on the end of her pen, she giggles and circles something in her notebook.

"You get anything I'm saying?" Jeff asks quietly. "Anything at all?"

I lift my chin to the assistant at the end of the stage. "Next," I call out.

[5]

Sometimes, it's the hardest thing just to get out of bed. The world is heavy and horrible, and all that heaviness and horribleness keeps you buried in your mattress and your sheets and your pillows, refusing to let you go when the alarm clock goes off.

This Friday is not one of those days. As if shot with a canister cocktail of adrenaline, caffeine, sugar and fucking fairy dust, I'm dressed in an instant and on campus half an hour early. I check my emails in seven minutes. I'm in class waiting for my students to show up and it's barely nine thirty.

Nine forty-seven, the first of my students trickle in. They stop talking when they see I'm already here, and I graciously ignore them and grant them due privacy as they silently take their seats. The students, a few at a time, some by themselves, slowly fill the seating area until approximately ten o'clock when all my students are here.

All of them except Justin Brady.

I wonder if I should dare wait for him. My insides are worked up. I'm not in total denial; I know that the reason for my excitement this morning and my sudden love for Monday, Wednesday, and Friday morning classes has everything to do with that hot fucker. I press my lips together, pensive, frustrated. Then, I'm instantly angry that all of this buildup, all of this excitement this morning was for nothing.

With a huff, I rise from my seat and, keys jangling in hand, I move toward the black box doors to lock them. Just as I reach for the handle, it swings open and he stands before me.

Justin Brady lifts his brows. "Am I late?"

I stare at his beautiful face for a second too long, startled, heart racing. Then I say, "In."

With a short, under-his-breath chuckle, he grins and enters the theater. I shiver as his aroma wafts past me, intoxicating me with whatever deodorant or body spray he's got on.

I return from the door, hiding the furious joy that's become of my heart, and reclaim my seat. "Alright, let's begin," I say right away, pulling my notebook onto my lap ... at just the same time Justin's shoes come to rest on the back of the chair next to me, inches from my head. I can even smell them. I ignore it.

My hardening cock can't. "Who's up first?"

A bony guy in the front row who I might or might not have seen in auditions hops to the stage, beating another guy there from the second row. He says his name and begins his piece, something from a Pulitzer Prize-winning play from six or seven years ago.

"You're chewing your words and I believe you as much as if you'd told me you were an orangutan," I tell him when he's done. "Next."

Next person, a thin guy with glasses and a striped shirt, performs a gripping piece I've heard ninety times. By "gripping" I mean it makes me want to throw up the breakfast I didn't eat.

"Too stiff," I tell him after he finishes with a look on his face that suggests he just delivered the greatest soliloquy the world has ever heard. I don't live for the look of collapsing joy on my students' faces, but I will admit it gives me a certain dark pleasure.

Next student finishes, I say, "Six seconds too long."

Another one finishes, I roll my eyes and say, "You slap your thighs every single time your hands drop. Stop slapping your thighs, we're not puppies you're trying to beckon."

Then, quite suddenly, Justin Brady decides to go next. He hops down the steps and to the acting area, and suddenly I'm *his* puppy, eyes on him with every ounce of focus I've got.

"Justin Brady," he tells us, his eyes bright and keen. "*Swag* by Bobby Fischer."

He didn't pick a new piece. Then, as if he took all my notes from last time and threw them out a window, I watch with a tightening gut as Justin works himself out of his shirt—once again—then tosses it to a dude in the front row. The class goes into another wave of gasps and giggles.

I open my mouth to say something, and for some reason, for some really humiliating, deep, unspeakable reason, the words die on my lips and I'm left breathing hoarsely, mouth parted, staring.

"All the boys look at me," he starts. He's looking at the dude in the front row, delivering his speech to him. It's all the same, as if he's replaying the show he gave us Wednesday. "They look and, like, all they see is just another hot shit clubster. But I'm ... more than that, bro. I'm more than what you see. I'm smart and I'm caring. I'm generous and, if any of those other boys think they can be me, I'll tell you what, they got big shoes to fill because ... I got *swag*."

Finished, he grins, looks up at me.

I'm pretty sure I know how ridiculous my face looks, but Justin has no reaction to it except to grin his sexy, wet smile and wait for whatever critique I dare give his flawless body and his prizewinning face and his—his—his nipples.

But we're not here to critique his body. "You did the same piece," I remark coolly.

"Yeah."

I lick my lips and stare at his shoulder for a moment. "You did the same piece and you took off your shirt again and … and you basically didn't listen to a single thing I said."

"But I spoke it all to one person," he says, his voice lilting with innocent defense.

"Yes. A guy in the front row."

Justin frowns cutely. "So … that's who my words are directed at. A guy."

"In the play, the character is saying those words to another guy?" I ask him, part serious, mostly facetious. "Is your character gay?"

Justin gives it two seconds of thought, then shrugs. "Yeah, sure. I'm not afraid of gays."

The class titters again. Every exchange between Justin and I in front of everyone feels like an argument with countless words between every line. Each tense statement and question is laced with a double meaning that I doubt either of us catch.

"Did you even read this play? *Swag*?" I ask him challengingly.

He ruffles a bit, shrugs. "Sure."

"Tell us what this 'play' is about."

"It's about ..." He searches for the words, his lazy eyes wandering across the class full of his amused or excited or otherwise turned-on peers. "It's about a cool guy searching for his inner swag."

"Yeah? Where does he find this swag?"

"He had it all along." Justin grins, thinking himself smart.

"*Swag* by Bobby Fischer," I say, feeling smarter. "Famous chess player Bobby Fischer? Or some made-up playwright? Some made-up play?" To that, he has no answer. "You trying to make a mockery of this class, Mr. Brady?"

"No, teach. It's just a—"

"*Professor Kozlowski.*" At my correction, he draws silent, his face resting with nothing more to utter. He only smiles dopily, all his sexiness still on display, pink nipples and all. "You've just flunked this simple first monologue, Mr. Brady. Your good looks and charm won't save you in my class. Take your seat."

He thinks for a moment, then says, "But you're saying I *do* have good looks and charm?"

The class chuckles, finding him all cute and endearing and sexy as a demigod. I let them have their moment. "What I'm saying," I say when they're through, leaning forward, "is: checkmate, Mr. Brady."

The laughing ends. Justin reclaims his shirt, slips it over his head, then lifts his eyebrows at me, curious.

"Checkmate," I repeat. "Take your seat." Without further prompt, he hops back up the stairs, whipping past me in a rush of whatever horribly enticing aroma he's got, and sits.

Then I say: "Next."

The rest of the students finish their pieces, a surprising amount of them forgetting their lines utterly and having to be prompted by a friend with the script. One student even tries to bring the script with him to the stage; I set him straight with a word and a roll of my eye.

I've filled my notebook with tiny notes and grades. I stare at the "F" I marked next to Justin's name long and hard, furious with it for some reason. He is failing; no doubt about it. He will flunk this class if something doesn't change. I distractedly dismiss the students and listen to the noise as they leave. Justin Brady goes too, laughing at something someone says to him, never paying me another second of mind. I watch his arms bulge as he grips his backpack, swinging it over a shoulder and vanishing out the theater door.

My gut stings with anger. I'm quite certain he's going to withdraw from the class. He's had his fun. He's played his game. Now it's over, and who the fuck knows who's won.

*Stale*mate, more like.

I vanish into my unlit office, dropping my notes on the desk and sighing, long and tiredly. Drawing myself to the glow of the computer screen, I skim through emails with watery eyes. Auditions. Auditions. Meeting next Monday. Auditions. I rub my face aggressively and pull my notes from last night's auditions in front of me, pulling it from a stack I'd made by my lamp right next to the calendar—Hey, two weeks and it's already Thanksgiving. I can't see what I've written, the computer screen being my only light. I've cast every role but one.

It's difficult to focus when all I'm thinking about is a cocky smile and pink nipples.

The official cast list for my spring show is supposed to be posted tonight, but I'll take the weekend and post mine Monday; that's sure to torture the students. The Head of the Theatre Department adores me, so I'm sure she'll allow it. "Everyone deserves a bit of a break," I tell myself, lifting the sheet off the desk and letting the light spilling in from my opened door illuminate the names better.

That's when I notice someone standing at the door. I drop the sheet and narrow my eyes. Against the dark, all I see is a silhouette.

"What do you want?" I ask, squinting, not even sure who the hell I'm talking to.

"It's dark in here," he says. "Can I ... turn on your light?"

"Who are y—?"

My words are cut off when the light switch flips and the freshman from my worst dreams and best nightmares stands in the doorway. His backpack hangs limp from his hand, dragging on the ground, and his eyes are on me, brow lifted to form those innocent wrinkles up his forehead.

"Hope I'm not, uh ... disturbing you," he says.

"Mr. Brady." His name sneaks from my mouth hesitantly, all the mistrust in the world dripping from those four meek syllables. *What is he doing in my office?*

Justin steps in, his eyes surveying the room as if he's looking for something. His eyes pry.

They're smart, sharp, poking into every shelf, jabbing at every drawer, just by the drifting of his simple, quiet, unassuming gaze.

"You want to tell me why you're here?" I blurt out, annoyed, unable to stand another second of his eyes brushing back and forth across my office, invading my space.

"Wanted to talk." He's still looking around.

"Have a seat," I say coolly, "and talk."

Distractedly, he sits in the chair across from my desk, his eyes still gazing across the room. I feel so encroached upon. I feel so ... strangely naked. What is Justin Brady doing here in my office?

"I ..." he starts, licking his lips. Just the simple act of him licking his lips is slow, deliberate, perfect. My eyes are drawn to them now, focusing on his lips as he slowly forms words. "Uh ... I was talking to my parents about tuition and like ... and how much classes cost and ..." He licks them again, turns his head to gaze somewhere else in my office. "I was hoping we could talk about, uh ..."

"About your failing my first assignment," I finish for him, speaking to his lips. "About how if you withdraw this late in the semester, you'll lose your money. That's not my problem."

"But, wait ... Hear me out," he says.

"You haven't cared about my class since day one, Mr. Brady. I think you and I both know that to be true."

"I care," he insists, his hazel eyes burning, reminding me of my recurring wet dream. "I'm just ... I'm just really bad at this acting stuff and I was thinking that, like ..." He peers up now, studying the ceiling as though it were some fascinating constellation in the night sky. "Maybe you could give me, like ... I dunno. Another shot, maybe? I mean ... Never really acted before. I'm new to this whole thing. And like, I thought maybe ..." He licks his lips. "I thought ..."

"You want me to cut you slack?" I scoff at him. "Like you're some exception to the rules I put on all my other students? You think you deserve special treatment, Mr. Brady?"

Now his eyes meet mine, and the effect is staggering. It was one thing to have his attention in the classroom among all the other students; it's entirely another for him to be seated in such close proximity to me, within this cramped office, and virtually alone. I'm so taken by the intensity of his keen eyes that I actually draw back an inch, as if afraid of something, as if afraid he can *see* the desire I've unhealthily nurtured for him.

Ugh, listen to that: *desire*. I never fucking use words like "desire" ... not even in acting.

"Would you give me another chance?" he asks, ignoring my questions. "I know I can do better. Promise to keep my shirt on this time." At that, he grins, thinking himself clever and funny and whatever.

"The 'F' I gave you has more to do with than just what you're wearing—or *not* wearing."

"Can you teach me?"

"Teach you what?"

He leans forward, propping his elbows onto his muscular thighs, which his tight designer jeans hug lusciously. "I wanna learn more about the art of acting. I feel so ... *behind* all the others in class. Do you get me, teach?"

I frown, suspicious. "If you feel so *behind* them, perhaps it'd help you to sit *in the front*. The back row is for people who don't care."

"The back row is also for people who do." He licks his lips; I can't help but watch. "I care, teach. I sit in the back so I can see everyone and learn everything. I hate to ... miss out."

The way he says "miss out", I feel an unspoken second meaning, as if he's trying to tell me something else. Or maybe I'm reading too much into it. Maybe I'm projecting, just *hoping* there are other things I'm meant to hear between his slow, sultry words.

"What is it, exactly, that you're asking of me, Mr. Brady?"

He lifts his eyebrows, wrinkling up his forehead adorably. "I just thought maybe you could ... teach me more about acting."

"That's what the class is for. You attend my classes to learn about acting. You don't come to my office with your tail between your legs because I gave you an 'F' and ask to learn about acting *here*."

"I just wanna suck less." He chuckles, his eyes light and blameless, and he licks his lips once more as he brings his harmless hazel eyes to mine. "You're a good teach, I can tell."

Why do I get the feeling he's a better actor than he's letting on? Why do I get the hunch that he's still playing me?

Why am I welcoming the fuck out of it?

I abruptly get up and come around the desk. "I have a cast list to fill and a lot of work to finish." My palms are a sweaty mess. "Come to class on Monday with a new piece—and your shirt on—ready to learn, and we'll see about making a proper actor out of you."

Justin rises from his chair, and his eyes are perfectly level with mine. Strange, how I haven't realized we're the same height until now. It's oddly sobering, to equal the height of someone so much younger than me.

I own you, something deep within whispers.

With his clever eyes burning, I feel my heart racing and my mouth going dry. He wears a smirk that suggests he's far more in control of this exchange than I even know. In the subtle curve of his boyish lips, he seems to grasp how very much he's got me wrapped around his finger, whether I admit it or not.

He extends a hand. "Thanks, teach."

With great reluctance, I allow him mine and shake his hand.

Justin looks down, perplexed suddenly by our clasping hands, and he doesn't let go. His brow wrinkling, curious, he says, "You have very soft hands."

"What?"

I tug, but he keeps firm grasp of my hand. "Do you use some kind of lotion, or ...?"

"N-No." I swallow, flinching and antsy. Justin Brady, with his deep intensity, seems to study my hand, turning it over, feeling it as they clasp. Then, ever slightly, he lets go and starts to examine my palm like a damn palm reader. He runs his fingers down it, transfixed.

My breath has become jagged. My heart is pounding against my chest so hard, I literally worry on whether I have the paramedics on speed dial. Why am I letting him do this? Am I *that* lonely? Has it been so long since I've had anyone in my life?

Well, yes. Yes, it has. Eight years, in fact. Eight fucking years of school and work and school and work and more school. Nothing but broken dates, canceled dates, nightmarish dates and nothing. I am one lonely, bitter, hardened, sad motherfucker. A sad motherfucker who is literally getting his hand stroked by a freshman in hot jeans.

Why don't I realize this isn't normal?

"Give me back my hand," I finally find the courage and willpower to say.

"I'll give it back when I'm ready," he says almost sweetly.

I yank, finally slipping it from his own. He looks up at me, meeting my eyes. Something is going on here and I'm not sure I trust it. I move to the door, gripping its handle. "I'll see you

Monday, Mr. Brady." I say it dismissively, prepared to shut the door when he goes.

He does not go. He just stands there, his lips curling and curling until suddenly his teeth are showing. The wider his grin spreads, the deeper the chill that lances down my body.

"Are you sure you can't give me lessons?" he asks again, stupidly, stubbornly ... sexily.

"You're taking my class," I repeat, just as stupidly. "You're already *getting* my lessons."

"Private lessons."

I stammer, unable to produce another word, wondering what he means by "private lessons" and what, exactly, those might entail.

He points out, "We got all weekend."

He has to be punking me. This whole thing is a joke to him. He's figured out I'm into him and now he's taking full advantage. And I'm ...

"What sort of lessons?" I ask.

And I'm letting him.

"Maybe I could meet you somewhere," he suggests, giving an innocent shrug. "Then you can give me some pointers. I wanna do good in your class. Maybe there's an actor in me somewhere." He shoves his hands in his pockets again, his biceps bulging in protest.

I'm all too aware of those biceps bulging in protest when I say, "Where would we even meet?" *What the fuck am I doing?*

"I don't know. Somewhere private where I could maybe ..." His tongue runs along his lips, thinking, though I imagine he knows exactly the effect his innocent licking has on me. "Where I could let loose," he decides to say.

Is he waiting for me to invite him to my place? Is that what's happening here? This isn't right. I should cut him off now, turn him away.

"608 Limestone Creek, two blocks east of the museum district," I tell him. "There's a ... a park near where I live. Plenty of space and—"

"Can we just do it at your place?"

He's really getting to the point. A hundred thoughts cross my mind all at once, turning my mind into a shockwave of fears and hopes and reasoning. I realize, Mr. Harrington *has* given voice lessons at his home before. I know singers who give lessons out of their home, too. It's not unheard of. Maybe this Justin Brady character just straight up, legit wants to learn more about acting. Maybe today humiliated him and he's really super great at hiding it.

I'm probably projecting all my sexuality onto him when, in reality, nothing at all is going on. Treat him like a student, don't treat him like the gourmet dish of strawberry-kiwi bisque that you're turning him into.

What the fuck is strawberry-kiwi bisque? "We'll do it at my place, then," I agree quietly. "512 Limestone Creek, just down the road from the ... from the aforementioned park."

"Cool." Justin's face softens, his eyes turning warm and his body squirming with relief. "Thanks, teach. When can I show up? Tonight? Around 8, maybe?"

"No," I say. "No time. I have obligations. Tomorrow morning."

"But I have nothing else today. Your class is my only one Fridays. Please, teach, can we do it tonight?"

Mr. Harrington himself told me quite recently—in auditions yesterday, in fact—that I need to just go for it. His words. The voice guru said I keep making excuses, holding back, that I just need to ... *let go.*

But what, exactly, am I letting go of? "Your private lessons begin tonight," I say. "Be there at 8 sharp. I don't like to wait."

[6]

I'm home five hours earlier than usual.

I clean off the coffee table and shove everything into the top drawer of my desk, figuring I'll go through it another time—as in, never.

I throw the dirty dishes into the dishwasher even though it doesn't work, just to get them out of sight.

I make my bed and pull clothes off the floor, thrusting them into my hamper without checking to see which are clean or worn.

I'm in full-blown sweat by the time I pull out the vacuum and give it a good run across the living room and down the hall. *I should invest in hardwood floors*, I tell myself.

Out of breath, I pull dust rags over every countertop and tabletop. I wipe my forehead and absently leave a huge clump of dust there, which I discover half an hour later when I clean the bathroom and catch sight of myself in the mirror.

"What the fuck're you doing?" I ask the sweaty man in the mirror.

Then I clean more. Washing the toilet on my knees, I consider what sort of lesson I can give him when he comes over. I can't do anything he'll be doing in class anyway. I doubt he'll have a new piece, so we'll probably have to work with his made-up, abominable "Swag" piece. Or maybe we can pick something from my selection and he can just do it on-book.

I take a shower and give myself a pep talk afterwards. I'm experiencing all these strange emotions, worrying on what to do with my hair, or what to wear, and it reminds me of my time in college, which suddenly doesn't feel like all that long ago. I try to fix my hair in that way where it looks like I don't care; it takes a lot of care to make it look like I don't care.

I put on a t-shirt and loose-fitting jeans, then check myself in the mirror. I want to look exactly enough don't-give-a-shit, as if I'd cared so little that I forgot he was coming over. I want to be pleasantly surprised at 8 PM when he shows up. Maybe I ought to be baking something. No, that would require me learning how to bake.

Is it so crazy that, even for teaching for years and having so much experience in college with expressing my art and regurgitating words and technique, that the thought of some private in-home acting lesson freaks me out? I wonder if I'd feel this way with any other student.

Or is it just the idea of Justin Brady in my house that makes me lose sanity?

An hour later, I'm cleaned up, dressed and sitting on my couch watching TV. Well, I suppose it's more accurate to say there is *something* on TV, but what I'm really watching is the clock hanging on the wall near it, a clock that reads 7:29 PM. I watch it with the intensity of a hunter, every minute dropping from the wall like another innocent bird that did nothing wrong, falling into the endless green below. Minute by minute, crawling by so slow that I cringe with anticipation and suck my tongue with impatience.

By 7:37 PM, I bring a laptop to the couch and feign calmness, browsing my Facebook and skimming the dumbest shit in my newsfeed. Mostly, videos of cats.

7:43 PM comes and I've tossed my laptop to the opposite side of the couch, throwing my head back and staring at the ceiling. The sound of a studio audience laughing and laughing fills the room. Punch line, studio laughter. Punch line, laughter. Actors saying lines, people acting like the actors are funny. It's all the same. It's all fake. I'm the same, I'm fake, I'm sitting here on this couch pretending not to be nervous.

Justin Brady, my one and only audience member. I hope he buys my performance.

7:49 PM and there's a knock at the door.

I literally hop off the couch and am on my feet like a cat at the sound of a vacuum cleaner. My eyes wide, I feel my mouth turn into a pot of sand. *I've made a mistake,* I tell myself. *This was a mistake. I've let my cock make an important decision for me. When have I ever let my cock have a say in important decisions?* I force my feet to bring me to the door. I take a deep breath. I take a deeper breath. I open the door.

Some stiff kid's standing there with a book. "Hello there, sir. Do you have time to speak about our Lord and Savior?"

I gape. I've nursed half a boner in my jeans, there's images of pink nipples dancing between my ears and a kid's at my door wanting to tell me about baby Jesus.

"I won't take up much of your time," he assures me, reading my expression. "I just want to discuss with you—"

"It's 8 at night!" I blurt out.

"God never rests," he assures me with a smile, gripping his book—his *bible*—tighter.

"Joke's on you," I spit back. "I'm gay."

"A true Christian embraces and loves his gay neighbors."

Great. A gay-friendly Christian and a bible at my door on a Friday eve, and *I'm* the asshole.

"To be really honest," I say, "I'm expecting company. Do you mind, like, coming back in a week or something? Then you can talk to me all about your baby Jesus."

"God bless," he says, then leaves. I watch him go, then shut the door and, with a tired sigh, I return to my couch and stare blankly at the TV. For some reason, that little exchange at the door just broke all my nervousness in half. I feel eerily calm and wonder if the whole world's punking me, or if bible boys really do visit houses this late in the evening on a Friday night.

The next time I bother to look at the clock, it's 8:07 PM. I experience a sudden sinking feeling in my stomach. At first I think, *Maybe he's lost.* I think, *Maybe he doesn't drive and he had to get a ride, and maybe his ride fell through.*

Of course, the more obvious thing is, maybe I've been stood up. Maybe he was never really serious, and he's already dropped my class and I'll never see him again. Already, I'm a puddle in his stupid, freshman hands. A fool. Mr. Brady is making me wait, if he's making me wait at all.

8:13 PM and the world still turns.

When the exact minute of 8:40 PM touches the clock, I turn off the TV and lie down on the couch, studying the ceiling. I'm still so eerily calm, like nothing can touch me, not even another knock at the door. I feel the cool touch of my laptop resting beneath my left foot, reminding me it's still there.

I remember one time back in college when I was waiting in the rehearsal room for my acting partner to show up, a semi-attractive guy with whom I was quite excited to be doing a scene. It was something between childhood friends from a boring-ass play, but I was so excited to act with him. I waited and waited for an hour and fifteen minutes. I waited more.

I remember the long walk back to my dormitory, furious that he'd not come to rehearse. When I grabbed lunch on the way back, I snapped at the server, feeling entitled to be rude and horrible because my wonderful, highly-anticipated rehearsal never happened. The sinking feeling in my chest that day, if only I knew it'd never leave me.

Every disappointment I experienced after that, it just added to the weight. Each cast list I looked at that didn't have my name. Every time my directors criticized me in front of the cast. Each victory that someone else experienced that I could've had.

I'm about five foot nine and weigh about a hundred and forty pounds, but sometimes the weight of disappointment that has dragged behind me over the years makes me feel like I weigh four hundred. I think that's the weight that keeps me from getting out of bed on the weekends. If I didn't have shows to direct, I'd probably sleep the whole weekend through. I'm such a depressing, miserable person.

Fuck it. I want pizza. I push myself off the couch, pull my phone off the kitchen counter and call the local delivery. A handful of minutes later, I trust some teen on the other end of the line with my credit card info and a pizza is now on its way to my humble abode. I pull a bottle of beer out of the fridge, pop it open and take a swig. I haven't kicked back a bottle in months; I've lost track. The familiar, bitter sting takes my mouth and throat, seeming to blur my eyes instantly.

My doorbell dings me at 9:22 PM when I'm drinking my third beer. I strut to the door, proud of the night I'm about to have, and swing it open to greet my dinner.

Justin Brady stands there instead.

My eyes right themselves and my lips part. Justin is wearing a snug black button-down and jeans, bunched up around his signature red-and-white high tops. His hair's styled perfectly, spiky and flipped up in the front as though he'd come from a fucking salon. He's a model, hopped right off the cover of a magazine.

And I'm quite suddenly very self-conscious of the beer in my hand. "J-Justin," I finally manage to say.

"Had a tough time getting here," he says. "Missed the bus and had to walk six blocks to catch another one. I'd call you to pick me up, if I had your number." His high cheekbones are flushed adorably, his hazel eyes shining and his teeth so white it hurts to look at them. "You gonna let me in?"

"Yeah. Yes." I step aside, letting in my guest. My heart pounds, pounds, pounds.

Just like in my office, I watch as he looks around, turning his head left, right, up. His eyes drink in my little house. The kitchenette to the right. The living room straight ahead. The blunt hallway to the left that leads to my bedroom, the spare room, and a bathroom. His eyes drink it all in in a matter of seconds.

I shut the door. He turns to me, his eyes bright and curious. I have just under three beers in me and I never drink. The effect this has on my decision-making process is one I fear.

"Ready for your lesson, then?" I ask, setting whatever's left of my bottle on the kitchen counter. I stumble over the change from tile to carpet as I move to the living room. I swear I'm not as think as I drunk I am. "We're going to start off with your horrible monologue."

"Can I have a beer?"

I look up at him, incredulous. "You invite yourself over for private lessons, and now you want me to promote underage drinking?"

He shrugs. "Legal age is eighteen in most countries."

"Legal age is 'none-of-my-students' where I'm concerned," I spit back. "Are we going to keep discussing legalities, or may we begin with the lesson?"

His eyes on me, fierce and piercing, I watch as he slowly, patiently leans against the kitchen counter. I'm confused until he reaches for the half-empty beer I'd left there. With a firm grip, he brings the bottle to his perfect, puckered lips, takes a swig, then meets my eyes again, a smug look of victory on his model boy face.

"My beer," he says, and those two words send a white-hot chill down my body, straight to my cock.

"I ... I didn't—I don't condone that."

But Justin Brady couldn't give two fucks. He kicks the bottle back again, deliberate, and this time, his eyes stay on mine, staring at me from around the bottle that hangs upside-down at his mouth. When he's done, he taps the bottle with a fingernail—*tap, tap, tap*—then says, "Why don't you get me another?"

I laugh. It might be the first time I've laughed in months. I recover and say, "You've got to be kidding me."

"Nah," he decides, tapping the bottle again. "I want you to get me another."

"What do I look like? Your bitch?" I laugh again at the gall of this sexy-as-fuck freshman in my house. "Here to do what you say?"

"Pretty much," he says.

Then, we both laugh. There's a twist of doubt in my gut though, because I can't quite tell if he's kidding or not.

"Alright," I mutter, playing the part. I come around the couch and take the empty beer from him. His eyes *never* leave me, watching my every move. Our fingers touch for a second when I take the bottle, and it makes me shiver. Ignoring said shiver, I deposit the bottle into the recycle bin, then grab another from the fridge. Bringing it to Justin, I humor him and say, "Want me to open it for you, too?"

He says, "Yeah, I do."

I pop open the beer, then hand him the bottle. He takes it from me and, never breaking his intense stare, he kicks back the beer and chugs, chugs, chugs. The way his throat works to swallow, the muscular way his lips connect to the bottle, it gives him such an air of dominance. It's like he's consuming me, chug by chug. It's like he's ... *swallowing me whole.*

He sets the bottle back on the counter, half-drank, then focuses on me for far too long without saying a thing. I resist my usual urge to express or break the awkward silence and just let it happen, returning his stare.

Then, quite abruptly, he breaks from the counter and moves to my couch. A strange confidence has filled him from toe to spiky hair. I don't have to be some expert in body language or a movement professor to see the command and authority in just his strut. *Maybe you're an actor after all,* I muse.

He turns his head, peering at me over his shoulder. An eyebrow lifted, he says, "Lesson starts over here, teach."

Lesson? Has he forgotten who's teaching whom?

"Over here," he says, like I'm a puppy.

And, just like a puppy, I ignore my own indignance and come to the couch. He sits. I sit. He props his feet up on the couch, shoes and all, placing them right by my hips.

I frown. "Your feet are on my clean couch."

"They're not clean enough for you?" He throws an arm over the back of the couch. Those bright high tops make his feet appear huge. "You hurt my shoes' feelings. Maybe you should rectify this situation of ours."

Whenever he uses certain words, trying to make himself sound smart and self-important, I feel a tinge of thrill. He's adorable, yet so hard and self-assured, even for looking like half a hot shit. He acts like a man twice his size.

"Oh? Your shoes feel bad now? How am I gonna rectify this?" I ask, amused.

He lifts his right foot. "Kiss it."

I stare at his shoe, then back at him. "You fucking crazy?"

"Kiss it. C'mon." He giggles, lifting his foot closer to my face.

I knock it away. He's obviously dicking with me. "What're you doing?"

"Commitment, isn't that what you said? In class? Gotta commit to our characters? I got commitment. Where's yours?"

I squint at him. Is he seriously using my lessons against me? "So what you're trying to say is, I'm playing a role right now, and you're playing a role, and you want me to commit to ... apologizing to your shoe."

"I can be a good actor." He grins.

Are we just messing around? Is this funny for him, or really some kind of exercise in roles and commitment? Is he amused, getting off on bossing around his professor who just gave him an 'F' for his first assignment?

Or is this payback? "I'm not kissing your shoe, Mr. Brady."

"If you don't kiss it," he says gently, "then my shoe is gonna be sad. And I can't have sad shoes." He pouts his bottom lip.

The thought grips me suddenly, of being beneath his feet. He's the hottest guy I've ever let near me since *my* first year in college; why the hell should I deny myself?

He could force my face onto his shoe, but I know the psychology behind this: he wants me to make the decision to submit to him. Just that realization sends a wave of twisted pleasure and humiliation through me, stirring all my guts. He wants to own me. *Just like your dreams.*

Blah, blah, reasons, blah. I kiss his shoe.

I watch as a grin spreads across his face, his blinding white teeth showing. He *loves* this. His cheeks redden and he won't stop grinning. "Oh muh gad," he murmurs. "Kiss it again."

"No fucking way."

"Kiss it again. C'mon. It's still sad, I can tell."

These red-and-white high tops that have defiantly rested on the back of the seat near my head all semester, these shoes that have, all this time, been a symbol of his dominance ... he's making me *kiss* them. I pucker up and kiss the tip, this time lingering a bit longer with my lips pressed to the rubber. Maybe it's the alcohol, maybe it's the strange dream state I'm in, but I feel my inhibitions slipping and *I don't mind.*

I hear Justin let out a tiny sigh—maybe a laugh—and then he moves his right foot in my face. "The other one, too. He feels left out."

After giving him one half-amused look of my own, I kiss his other shoe. I realize that this is giving me a very, very, *very* hard erection. It aches, cramped up inside my briefs and pants.

"You're really into this," he says, my lips still locked on his right shoe like a lover. I pull off, about to say something to him when he snaps his finger and points. "Hey, hey, no! Don't stop! You're hurting its feelings again!" I put my lips back to his shoe. "Good, yeeeeah. There ya go." The grin returns to his face.

Is this what he wanted all along? Is he some kind of twisted dominant mind-fucker? Did he plan this whole thing for months, or is he improvising? Maybe he should enroll in my Improvisational Advanced Acting class. Who cares that he has none of the prerequisites.

Then I hear a snapping. My lips not leaving his shoe, I look up and pay witness to an award-winning performance called *The Hot Shit Slowly Unbuttons And Takes Off His Shirt*. When he works the snug shirt off his sleeves, his feet twitch a bit, shaken by his efforts, and his right shoe slaps me in the cheek, almost like it has a mind of its own, and I continue to kiss it while straining to watch.

When the shirt's off, he says, "Keep going."

I keep going. Then he puts his hands behind his head, his pits exposed, his staggering display of abs crunched and visible, and those pink nipples I'd *so* rather have my lips latched onto. I'll stay down here as long as he wants me to, but I want to be up there admiring the rest of him so badly, so fucking badly.

But, nope. He wears that shit-eating grin, his hands behind his head, and all that sexy model boy muscle is so far out of reach that it's like my cramped cock is trying to grow harder and harder and harder, as if it could reach it if it got erect enough. No, cock, it doesn't work that way, you're just making me more and more insane with horniness and desperation.

I pull my lips off his shoe with a sudden thought. "I'm expecting a pizza, by the way. Should be here any minute now."

He wrinkles his face. "What kind?"

"Pepperoni."

"Not stuffed-crust?" He sounds let down, as if I'd ordered the pizza for him. I give a shake of my head. "That's lame. Hey, what're your lips doing?"

"Talking," I answer.

"They need to be *kissing*. Hey, actually I think my shoes are fine now. All forgiven." He kicks them off with the quickest maneuvering I've ever seen. The thick boyish aroma of sweat wafts over my face as I stare at his giant socked feet. I feel the warmth of them, too. White socks, athletic, with red stripes and a brand name running up the side. I'm intoxicated instantly. I've never been into feet before, not like this. What the fuck is this cocky fuck doing to me?

"I know you're hypnotized and all that," he says with a fake "over it" roll of his eyes, "as my feet are admittedly pretty amazing, but you got a job to do. Make them happy."

For a second, I move to kiss them. The next moment, my face is buried in his feet, inhaling with such intensity it's like I wish to consume them. Without even knowing if it's okay, I grab his feet with my hands as if to massage them and I inhale again, gripping them tight and pressing my face into them.

"You fucking love this," I hear him say.

"Shouldn't have had three beers," I admit, muffled by his big socked feet. "I don't know what I'm doing."

"What was that?" he says. "Sorry, can't hear you with my big amazing fucking feet in your face."

I pull away. "I said—"

"Get your face back in there!" I push my face back into his feet, shutting up. "Damn. This is gonna be an easy semester. What was it you said to me? I'm not gonna get through your class based on my good looks and charm? Isn't that what you said?" He laughs. Just the sound of his laughter, each individual boyish burst of amusement from his chest, shoots a bolt of pleasure down my body. I wonder if I could cum just from the sound of his condescending, down-talking voice.

How can someone make me feel so small and yet so big at the same time? I'm like a scruffy little pet of his ... an object, a toy ... and yet I'm the most important thing to him right now. He makes me feel so ... *necessary.*

"Hey, teach," he says, his hands still behind his head, kicked back. "You like how it smells down there?"

I sit up, pulling my lips and nose out of the exhilarating domain of his feet and staring at Justin Brady. "This isn't how I thought your lessons would go," I admit.

"It's you who needs the lesson, methinks." He giggles, amused. "Come up here. I got something else for you."

With half a stagger and a bit of confusion as to where, exactly, he's wanting me to come up to, I move down the couch a bit, then find myself on my knees in front of the couch, pleasantly closer to his exposed upper body. My eyes slide down it like a buffet. Where the fuck do I start?

"You wanna touch it, right?"

"Touch what?"

"My body."

I'm stuck in my head. We're already gone past the point of no return. I can't undo what I've already done. He's got me. *He's got me.*

"Well, now you've hurt *my* feelings," says Justin, innocent and pouting his lip. "You don't wanna touch it?"

"I do," I blurt out.

"Too late. You've hurt my feelings. Now you need to apologize."

"I'm sorry."

"Do I have a name?"

"I'm sorry, Justin."

"That's not what you call me."

I have to think for a second before saying it. "I'm sorry ... Mr. Brady."

"Great. But words won't make it better." I wrinkle my face, not following. "I want you to apologize with your tongue."

I'm still confused. Then, as comprehension dawns on me, my whole body quakes with excitement. Is he seriously asking me to put my tongue on his body? There is no way this whole thing is just about degrading me; he *has* to be enjoying it too. No fucking way.

"I don't see any apologizing," says king of the couch, kicked back and ready to be served.

I open my mouth and touch my tongue to his ribs like a dog. Slowly, my tongue moves, tracing each rib. With a quick glance at Justin's face, I note that he's watching me with this sort of severity that suggests he won't be easily satisfied. He doesn't rock his eyes back. He doesn't moan. He just lies there with a smug curve to his lips, fire in his hazel eyes and fire upon his boyish cheeks. My tongue bathes his ribs one by one until, steadily, slowly, carefully, I reach his pec. That beautiful pink nipple I've dreamed about lies just before my wetted eyes.

Am I allowed to taste it? Am I really, truly allowed to do this?

Then, as if drawn by a magnet, my lips encircle his nipple and I suck. I suck and I twirl my tongue around it like a dance. It becomes hard in my mouth. I dare a glance at Justin and find he's still watching with that unaffected, smooth-as-stone face. He's a king and he's above showing me appreciation for my tongue, for my worship, for my attention.

Mighty fine with me; I'm reaping gold.

Gaining confidence, I lift myself to his other nipple, bracing myself with a hand on the back of the couch. Over Justin, I latch onto the other perfect, pink specimen. I feel deep and exhilarating satisfaction when it goes hard under my tongue. I give it a kiss, another kiss, and I'm suddenly making love to his nipple. He's not moaning, so I have to imagine it. I have to imagine that this is driving him crazy.

There's not a hair on his chest. He's smooth and supple and unflawed. I trace down his pec with my tongue like an icicle, bringing myself across his abs, kissing each one as I move lower, lower. Will he allow me ... *down there?*

I stop when my chin hits the button of his jeans. I look up to meet his cold, all-knowing eyes. Is this what he really wants? Does he ... *want* me to continue?

"Apology's not over," he says.

I take that for my permission. I grab the button of his jeans with two clumsy hands; you'd think I'd never undone someone else's pants before. When the button finally gives way, I pull his zipper down and listen to the delicious, gentle ripping sound of freedom. His underwear, white microfiber briefs, seems to withhold a very generous gift. I look up at him again, uncertain. I feel like I need him to say it outright and to not have me keep running on assumptions and half-words and euphemisms.

He lifts his eyebrows expectantly, waiting.

I grip the rim of his underwear and, ever gently, I pull. I pull slowly, I pull with the care of a lover's touch. The underwear gives to everything I hoped and feared it would. He is not small. *He is so, so, so not small.* I know that every porn in the world would promise something huge under the waist of the object of your affection, but when it happens in real life, it's a bit staggering.

Quite suddenly I've pulled the underwear too far, and his hard cock flips out so fast, it literally slaps me in the face. I jump, startled by it, and then Justin's laughing his ass off.

The moment shatters like a window from a brick. "Really, Justin?? You find it funny??"

"My," he says, laughing, "dick," laughs, "just bitch slapped you." He laughs and laughs. It's the funniest fucking thing in the world.

Let's see how much he's laughing in a second. I grip the base of his cock, long and thick, then wrap my lips around the tip. I have no confidence that I can manage more than half of his engorged manhood in my mouth, but I sure as fuck give it the effort it deserves. My opened mouth takes his cock, drawing it into my mouth, down my tongue, and into my throat. I pull up, managing only a few inches of it, then go back down. Up and down my mouth runs, sucking and bathing his throbbing meat with my tongue. For a while, I almost forget it's attached to a person. I give Justin a glance.

He's stopped laughing. With his lips parted and eyes wide, he watches me suck him off.

I come off his cock, give an insolent look of my own. "Forgiven, yet? Or does your precious body need more apologizing? I don't think—"

He shuts me up by doing half a crunch, gripping my hair and shoving my head back onto his cock without another word. I fight a gag reflex as he grips the back of my head, pulling me up and down his swelled dick as it invades and retreats from and invades and retreats from my throat, over and over.

Under any other circumstance, I would feel angry and I would fight him. I've never liked going down on any of my ex-boyfriends. It's my least favorite thing to do. I get pubes in my teeth. I gag too easily. I taste and smell things that turn me off. *Why the hell isn't this turning me off?* In fact, if anything, I've never been more turned on giving head in my life, even if it's half-forced. The dominance that Justin Brady exudes, the *strength* in his arms and his fingers as he grips my head and tells it where to go without words ... it gives my cock reason to throb and ache *worse* against the unforgiving material of my jeans and tight underwear.

"Tell me you're sorry," he says, pulling my head up and down and up and down the length of his cock. "Apologize to Mr. Brady and his big ol' dick."

I'd use my mouth to apologize, really, truly, but as there's something in it, I opt to twist my diffident, meek eyes to meet his. When they do, he grins wildly, all his teeth showing. He is enjoying this so much.

And so the fuck am I.

Suddenly, he sits up, pushes me back, and his big hands grip my face like a soccer ball, holding me in place. I'm confused and turned on and horribly inattentive. "I have an idea," he says, and I think those might be the scariest words I've heard all night. "I want you to do something. If you do it, you'll be all apologized. If you don't, I'm gonna be all sad again."

"What is it I'm—" Before I even get out the words, he grabs my hand and puts it on his hard-as-steel cock. Then, gently, he starts to move my hand for me, stroking his cock. I look up, meeting his eyes. "You ... want me to ...?"

He lets go, allowing me to take over, then kicks back and grins. "You're gonna keep your face right there, right in front of my dick, right in the line of fire. You're gonna jerk me off and, if you do a good enough job, you'll earn my 'forgiveness' that you want so much." He bites his lip, satisfied with himself.

Yeah, I'll earn his forgiveness alright; I'll earn his forgiveness all over my face. But I don't balk; I keep my hand moving, faster and faster. I watch him *try* to maintain a straight face, but I sucked him good and hard, and now I'm about to bring him over the edge. Despite the even face he's failing to keep, his breath starts to quicken, and I watch as his fingers curl, gripping the couch at the top and the bottom, tightening, tightening.

His cock pointed at my face like a gun, I'm milking him solid, knowing what havoc I'm inviting on my face. My heart pounds in my ears and, for never having laid a finger on my cock, I'm impossibly hard. I suspect the king of the couch gives zero fucks about that fact. Until he smiles, and maybe even after that, Justin won't give one wet, muscled fuck. The reward is on its way for him, but it's already here for me: I love being owned by the freshman.

"Almost forgiven," he breathes.

Yes, there's three beers in me, not even, but I'm really *not* drunk. I can't use alcohol as the excuse for my acts tonight. There's something else entirely that's moving my eager hand right now—a force, a hunger, a *desire* deep within that's fueling my need to worship every inch of Justin Brady's body.

"Almost," he growls. His eyes pierce me, powerful and furious. "Few more minutes."

Few more seconds, he meant. His cock turns tense as bone in my hand, seizing up, and I close my eyes as a wave of warm cum sprawls across my cheek. Another wave, covering my nose. A curtain flings across my forehead. Another misses my face entirely, lands on my shoulder. Another hits my chin, dribbles down. Yet another spills across my lips, giving me cause to moan.

In seconds, the cum feels cold on my face, and I open my eyes, thankful to any god that might have dared paid witness to this scene that Justin's "forgiveness" didn't blind me. He twists his head, eyebrows lifted, breathing heavy, and his lazy eyes lock onto mine. He starts to giggle stupidly. I smile, and his giggle turns into a full-blown laugh. A glob of his cum falls off my chin, lands on his thigh.

When he finally recovers, he nudges the side of my head with his foot. "What'd we learn today, teach?"

"Still trying to figure that one out," I admit. "Listen, I'm gonna … I'm gonna clean up." I stand up carefully and move toward the hallway, steering myself for the bathroom. He calls out to me, saying not to clean up, that I look so pretty with his jizz all over my face, but I ignore him. A washcloth finds my hand, my hand finds the sink, and then I bring it to my face and wipe away all that I can.

My mind is literally in a state of numbness. I don't even know what I'm feeling. I'm still insanely horny, yet my stomach is tugged with an untimely barrage of feelings and frustrations and woes. I don't even feel like getting myself off. I just feel …

"Teach!"

I come out of the bathroom, drawn back to the living room. He's still on the couch, but he's put his cock away and closed his jeans back up. His arm is over the back of the couch, the other gently stroking up and down his abs, invitingly. When he sees me, he chuckles, all his teeth showing.

I cross my arms, thinking on what I want to say. Then, quite suddenly, I blurt out, "Did you enjoy that?"

His eyes are so smart. His eyes have always been so smart, like he's a hundred steps ahead of me, all the time. I'm always the one ahead of my class; it's why I'm the professor, it's why I intimidate my students, it's why I have the reputation I do. How has this Justin kid gone and flipped it all around so easily? I don't know who I am around him.

"Yes, I did. Question is," he says, absently picking at something on the back of my couch, "did *you* get what *you* wanted out of this?"

"I'm ... not entirely sure what I wanted."

"Isn't that the lesson here, teach?" He laughs again, runs his hand up his abs—and I follow, I so, so, so follow that wicked hand as it reaches his nipple, giving it a little pinch. "We all play roles, don't we? I'm the hot guy in class you never had, aren't I? That's kinda the role I thought I was filling."

"You're not filling any *role*, Mr. Brady."

"Really? We're not on a first name basis yet? Seriously, I had my cock in your mouth, and I—"

"Justin." I let out a light chuckle. I find myself overcome with this whole circumstance. I never imagined this semester to start off like this. "I'm freaking out a little because ... I'm thinking about how you're my ... my ..."

"Don't worry about it. Flunk me. Pass me. Seriously, I just came over for the beer I didn't know you had and the mouth I didn't know was so ... skilled." He laughs, his wet teeth showing and his face flushing happily.

"Who the fuck are you?" I exclaim, but my tone is light, a smile breaking across my face.

He smiles too. Rising off the sweaty couch, ruined by our unabashed mischiefs, he grabs his shirt and flings it over a shoulder. "I'm the guy that just got off," he answers, proud of himself, then struts out of my house, pink nipples and all. The door closes softly behind him.

I remain, boner and all, the guy that did *not* just get off. I'm a mess of horniness. I'm still turned-on, even now. Something in what he said makes perfect sense, yet I can't say what. Something about the roles we play …

The hot guy I never had …

"Where's my fucking pizza??" I cry out.

[7]

I spend Sunday in the office when no one else is there at all. There's not even anyone in the computer lab, which is literally unheard of. The whole place is empty and I'm sitting in my office at my desk staring at my hands.

These hands gripped Justin Brady's cock.

These hands ran across his pure, muscular body. They touched his clothes.

They wiped his cum off my face.

I couldn't sleep at all Friday. I was restless all day and night Saturday. I couldn't even jerk off, couldn't get it out. Pent up, breathless, gutless, I stare at my hands and reimagine it all.

I hear the main door to the office open, somewhere out of sight around the corner. I stir, surprised that someone else is here. Belatedly, I recall the costume lady saying she had some scheduling conflicts to approve for the members of her costume crew and she might come in on Sunday to figure them out. Blowing it off, I stare back down at my hands. I imagine how much longer Justin's hands were ... how much bigger. *Justin Brady*, I can still hear myself whispering that night I jerked off to the fantasy of him.

Now, it's no longer a fantasy. It happened.

It ... sorta happened.

"Thom?"

I look up. Mr. Harrington's standing in the doorway.

"Justin," I say, surprised.

He seems as surprised. "Uh, sure, I *can* be." He smiles. He's not wearing his usual stiff clothes; he's dressed in a snug green v-neck that shows off his pecs, with white-blue jeans. He looks downright adorable in people clothes.

"What're you doing here on a Sunday?" I ask him, wrinkling my face.

He shrugs. "I got bored. Sometimes, can't stand my own company. Gotta get out of the apartment and … see what's up on a campus on a boring Sunday afternoon. Not so boring anymore, now that I've found you." He laughs, leans against my doorframe. His arms bulge, stretching the sleeves of his v-neck. *Why haven't I noticed these things before?* The only thing he's ever worn around me is plaid buttondowns, big sweaters, and pinstriped dress pants.

"I know the feeling," I confess. I give a sad, sideways nod at my computer. "I still haven't figured out my cast list. My head is all messed up and I have no idea what I'm going to do. No prospects, no hope, no nothing. Sundays suck. Some boy came by my house wanting to talk about Jesus. He was even down with the gays."

"It's a trap!" exclaims Mr. Harrington, and I have to laugh. "Hey, my name's Jeff by the way. Nice to meet you."

"Huh?"

"You called me Justin earlier."

"Oh." I frown, blushing. "I did?"

"Yep." He smiles again. He has dimples. Deep dimples. I feel like I've always known this fact, yet am just now allowing myself to see them. "But you can call me whatever you want, really. I've been called much worse. You might have a reputation with your actors, but I got one with my singers. Too bad, really. I like helping people find their voice."

"I think you helped me find mine," I admit. Sucking on my lips, I disallow myself from saying anything more, all my dirtiest, sickest, most guilty thoughts consumed with the boy in the red-and-white high tops I kissed. I stare down at my hands again, the culprits.

"Why don't we get a bite?" he asks, drawing my attention back to his cute face. "We're the only ones here, Thom. It's way too quiet to do work here, let's be honest."

"Let's be very honest," I agree, changing my mind about spilling nothing. "I need to be honest. I did a fucked up thing."

He giggles. "Now *this* I'd like to hear."

"I doubt it." The hands I'm trying to look at are shaking.

"Try me. Think I'm gonna judge you? Fuck that. You're the coolest person here, always have been. Try me." He comes up to my desk, puts himself in the chair across from it—the same chair freshman Justin Brady sat in when he convinced me to give him private lessons at my house. "Let's hear it."

"I messed around with someone."

He nods excitedly. "Yeah, definitely want to hear about this. Details. I want details."

I frown at him. I was expecting at least a tinge of jealousy. I'm not blind and stupid; I know Mr. Harrington's had a thing for me, I've known for a long time.

"Details?" I mutter.

"Yeah, let's hear it." His face is light, his eyes bright and inviting.

I get up and come around the desk, leaning against its front. "Well, it was someone I ... definitely should *not* have messed around with.

But I was a little drunk. I never drink, mind you, but I had a few beers this particular night. And I just ... I just ..."

"You let go," he finishes for me. My eyes find his, anxious, uncertain. "Nothing wrong with that, Thom. Don't be ashamed of being alive. C'mon."

"I feel skeezy, to be honest."

"You ought to feel *human*, Thom. We all get horny. We all get stupid, especially when we're horny. Stupid is kinda fun, really. So's skeezy. So's drinking. What you did is just being ... human."

"I acted a fool, Jeff."

He smiles, I guess because I used his first name and not his last for once. "Imagine that. The acting professor *acting* like something. Next you're gonna try to claim I sing."

Now I'm smiling. "Y'know, I have never actually *heard* you sing."

"It's terrible. I have no idea why they keep me employed. Can we get out of this dreary office, please? You still owe me a bite of lunch."

"Sing something." I lift my chin defiantly.

He bites his lip, pensive, curious. "So *that's* what we're gonna do, is it? I gotta sing for my date, is that it?"

"Sing your heart out."

And then he does. All the humor drops from my face as his eyes lock onto mine and his gentle voice makes music. I'm overcome as the lyrics drop from his lips, filling the office with shameless, uninhibited music from the filling and emptying body and throat and musical instrument that is Jeffrey Harrington.

When he finishes, the look on his face is strange, perplexing. "What?" he mutters, his crystal eyes on mine. "Was I that bad?"

I push off the desk, grip the arms of his chair with my hands, and plunge my face into his. When our mouths meet, it's tender and soft. He tastes sweet. He smells clean, freshly showered, and a trace of cologne on his neck hints to me that he cared today.

Suddenly he pushes out of his chair, our lips never disconnecting, and he pulls on my clothes like they're a puzzle. Our breath turning jagged, noses shoving air at each other's faces as we kiss maddeningly. We grapple with each other's stubborn shirts until they fall off, slipped over our heads or otherwise. He grabs at my pants, working the button as I do the same with his. Our eyes closed, we're grappling in the darkness together, even with the office half-lit. My hands on him, his hands on me.

Then we're on the floor and I'm staring down at him, a question on my face as I hover over him. My cock lingers by his ass, pointing, desperate. His left hand vanishes, wrestling with his jeans until he produces a wallet. From it, a single silvery condom packet drops out.

"This was planned?" I ask, teasing him.

"Always prepared," he says quite seriously.

Then a condom is rolled onto my cock and, as though we were never interrupted, I spit into my hand like a pro and awaken the lubrication on the condom, stroking myself. Flinging his legs over my shoulders, sensitive and slick as a motherfucker, I bring the tip of my cock to his ass and draw circles teasingly.

Out of breath he says, "I've wanted this for so long."

"It was a student," I blurt out. "I messed with a student. He was a touch aggressive, but we kind of pursued each other. I can't place the blame." My cock pushes into his ass quite suddenly, slipping in faster than either of us expected. I gasp with pleasure; he gasps with surprise. His eyes grow wide, brow lifted. "I imagine that changes everything," I whisper.

"I had a thing once with a student," he confesses back. "It happens. It's okay. It's—Oh god, this feels good."

I'm surprised. "Really? You? A thing with a student?—Who was it? When?"

"Well, no." Jeff laughs. "No, not really. I just made that up just now so you wouldn't feel alone. I'm so considerate, aren't I? Oh god." His eyes rock back as I fuck him slowly, my balls tapping his ass with each gentle thrust. "Harder. Do it harder, Thom. Go hard. Oh god. Tell me about the student."

"He was a cocky fucker." I thrust harder.

"Oh god. Tell me more." Jeff reaches up and grips my arms, nearly clawing at them. "Oh god."

I shiver, my pent-up cock tingling with the horny buildup of an entire weekend of fantasy and regret and longing. "He dominated me." I thrust hard. "He took control of me." I thrust harder, harder. "He owned me."

"Fuck, fuck, fuck." Jeff's drunken eyes meet mine, his drunken, smiling eyes. "How'd it feel, mister control freak, to lose all your control?"

I grip his shoulders and, each time I thrust my cock into him, I pull his shoulders down, pushing my cock deeper into him, deeper, harder. He's gasping now with every thrust, his firm body shaken by my every loving shove.

"It was freedom," I admit.

"Whole new role for you," he nearly sings, his voice lost as his breathing grows heavier, heavier. "Being owned. Oh, I'm close."

"I'm closer."

And then I cum inside him. With every

thrust, I yell out, all of my demons flying out of my mouth like little roars. I don't stop the thrusts, staring down into Jeff's eyes as his mouth opens wide. It's something like a gasp. It's something like a personal heaven. It's like a discovery, like a lesson, like a man who's just found his ... swag.

Jeff's cock erupts between our sweat-ridden bodies. I'm still fucking him, even while spent, fucking his cum out of him. He isn't as vocal as I was, his mouth open and his eyes seeing stars, though all he seems to look at is me.

I'm all he sees. His eyes smile, his face relaxing as the climax subsides. I drink in the sight of his satisfied face and wonder how such happiness, how this man under me, can lie under my nose for so long unseen. It just took a giving in for my stubborn eyes to open.

"You're pretty when you cum," I tell him. He smiles at that, those dimples of his showing in the dim office light, like two valleys of happiness in his face. "How was it for you?"

"Worth the wait," he confesses.

I collapse into him, drawing his body into my arms and embracing him. Neither of us seem to care about the sticky mess we've made between us. It's sort of beautiful, to make dirty such a clean, put-together person. There's a thrill in ripping control out of the hands of a person who is always so controlling. A natural balance and necessity to shoving a professor under the feet of a freshman. Sometimes, it's the teacher who needs the lesson.

Between us, one of our stomachs growl. I can't say with confidence whose it was. "How about that bite?" he murmurs in my ear.

"Sure," I say back. "*Anything* but pizza."

[8]

When I pass through the doors on Monday, I feel a lightness I haven't felt in years. I smile at the kids in the lobby and they have *no* idea what to make of it. I tell Gloria at the front desk that I love what she's done with her hair, not even certain she's done anything with it. I pass by Bill in the box office and wave at him, to which he returns a meek, hesitant wave.

The black box doors open and, though it's ten already, I decide to "forget" to lock them and, instead, I merely stroll to my seat among the students. They draw silent at my arrival. I take my seat and mind the faces before me.

Justin Brady, sitting in the front row, turns around and gives me a subtle lift of his brow.

I smile at all of them, Justin included. "I've decided to erase your grades for your first monologue attempts," I tell my students. "I'm doing something a little different this semester. You'll have a lifetime of judgment and bad auditions and rude directors ahead of you, so why teach you to fear them from the start?" I toss my notebook to the side; it lands with an unimpressive thud against the back of a seat, slides to the floor. "This class is going to be your home. Live in it. Get comfortable. Don't fear the stage; that's your home too. Don't fear your body because it's where all the roles you'll ever play live. Don't fear your voice because it's the voice of every role of life inside you. It's the mother and the father inside you. It's the job applicant. It's the confident man or woman you'll be on your next date. It's the C.E.O. of a company. It's ... the cocky freshman."

My eyes drift to a certain someone in the front row, whose hazel eyes glow with thought.

I nod at the stage. "New assignment. Get up there and perform your piece. Any piece. We're gonna have fun. We're gonna remind ourselves why we call them 'plays'. So get up there," I tell my students, "and play."

The next hour is spent watching my students live on the stage. Some of them don't get it right away at first, but soon, they start to take after one another. They find confidence. They find humor. They find looseness. I don't kid myself; none of them are exploding with stellar performances or moving me to tears, but the lesson today isn't to be perfect. It's to make a friend of fear. It's to make a home out of the stage. It's to own the stage before it owns you.

Or some shit like that.

"Thanks, Professor Kozlowski!" says one of the students on their way out. I return a muted smile. "See you Wednesday!" exclaims another, rushing through the door. I watch with bright eyes, wondering how long this delightful mood of mine will last. I can imagine myself already collapsing into a stew of misery, becoming my old, intimidating self by the end of the week. Who knows. I'm only human. I have to laugh at the ironies of my life, otherwise I'll have nothing left to laugh at. Besides, I have some plans with Mr. Jeff Harrington later and I'm in too good a mood to mind.

He lingers. I turn my eyes to him and I feel a tinge of anxiety touch my stomach. "Justin," I say rather cautiously, acknowledging him.

"Teach," he says, smiling back. "I uh ... I saw the cast list and, uh ... I kinda thought that maybe you would've, uh ..."

"You didn't audition," I tell him simply. "I can't put you in a play when I really don't know who you are as an actor. You're young and you're new to this. You said that yourself."

Justin shoves his hands into his pockets. He hides the smile on his face, looking at a spot on the ground. "I know. I'm only half-kidding anyway. I didn't *really* expect you to cast me in your spring play." He lifts his eyes. "I guess I was just wanting to be a part of something."

"You are. You already took the first step."

"What do you mean?"

"You enrolled in my class, Mr. Brady." I give a nod at the acting space. "You'll be up there the rest of the semester. You have time to grow. There's still the summer plays you can audition for early next semester, y'know."

"Yeah." He nods, a bit inspired by that thought. Then, with a lift of his eyebrow, he adds, "I guess I could learn a thing or two from you in the meantime."

I lean in and whisper, "I'm a better teacher without three beers in me."

Justin Brady studies me, trying to figure something out. His hair is more calm today, not flipped up like usual. Even the usual ferocity of his eyes seems somehow muted, underplayed.

I move to the doors of the theater, then hold them open for him. He hesitates only a moment, then moves through the doors. He stops in front of me, lifts his pretty gaze to me and says, "Y'know what I respect about you?"

I tilt my head. "What's that, Mr. Brady?"

He says: "You're fair."

I nod, appreciating that. "Thank you."

"And," he adds with a clever smirk, "I'm enrolled in Basic Acting II next semester." He gives me a wily flash of teeth. "Guess I care after all."

When Justin Brady leaves, I find myself watching after him. My notebook clung to my chest, I consider how fair I really am. Has the student changed me, or have I changed the student? I feel my heart beating against my notes of criticism, my grades, my F's and A's and B's, and I think about the roles we play. *I'm just the guy that got off*, he'd said the other night.

I'm left there in a curious daze, wondering whether the freshman owned me at all, or if perhaps it was I, all along, who owned him.

The end.

Printed in Great Britain
by Amazon